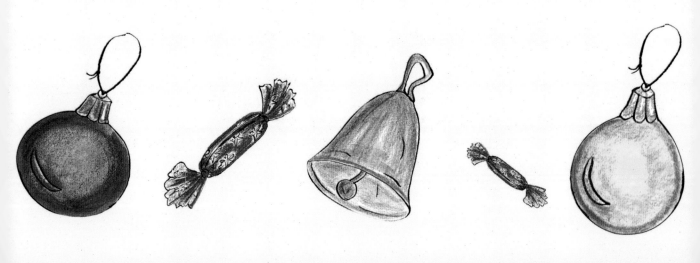

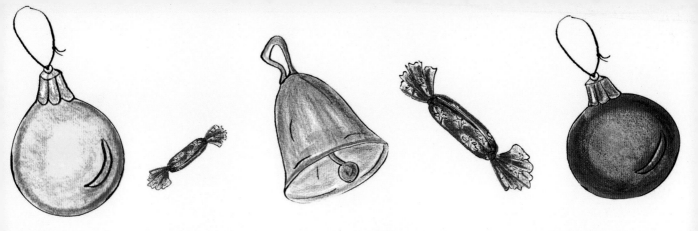

To the storyteller in each of us, and children of all ages
who love a new story

To my first and second generation Angels of God.
ILYMTYLM
ATTWIWABF

In loving memory of my dearest friend
Phillip Andrew Stallone
1989-2015

Welcome to the Fall Suitcase Stories

When author Peggy Dolan was 10 years old, she was already writing story poems and loved to read biographies of famous authors. During a trip to the bookmobile, she found a book about Emily Dickinson and was surprised to read that her work did not become notable until after her death, when it was found in an old trunk in the attic. That night at the supper table, Peggy asked her mom and dad if they had a trunk she could use for her poetry. That way, she could put it in the attic and if she died, her work could be as famous as Emily Dickinson. Her mom and dad said they didn't have a trunk or an attic, but she could use her dad's old World War II suitcase. There was a half-door in her bedroom that opened to an unfinished closet, so Peggy marked her suitcase with the words "The works of Peggy Dolan" and kept her suitcase there.

Peggy continued to write through grade school and filled her suitcase with poems and memorabilia of special events in her life. In eighth grade, she wrote a 108 verse poem about the assassination of John F. Kennedy on November 22, 1963. Her principal, Sr. Mary Esther S.S.N.D., sent Peggy to all eight grades in the school to read her poem to the students. Her writing skills in high school were encouraged by a teacher, Sr. Karl Mary S.S.N.D., and by senior year she earned the co-editor position of the school's paper, the *Rosary Links*. She wrote a poem in tribute to her brother's best friend, Sargent John David Beltz, who was 19 and was killed in Vietnam on November 4, 1966.

It was published in the local paper, and Peggy still keeps it and shares it while storytelling to children. After she became a teacher, she continued to write children's story poems. Her first was *Mitch the Mushroom As Told By A Big Old Fat Green Frog*. Her favorite, *Freddy the Christmas Snowflake,* was written to be used in the Christmas play that the entire school participated in—the same school that Peggy read her 108 verse poem about John F. Kennedy to back in eighth grade!

Freddy the Snowflake is included in Peggy's first Suitcase Stories series. Her old suitcase travels with Peggy to all of her storytelling engagements.

Some of her stories contain the names of her family or friends, and some are even based on actual events and things that really did happen. See if you can tell which poems are real and which are pure imagination. In the meantime, Peggy encourages students to write and collect memorabilia of special events that happen in their life. She sends students home with the idea to create or find a special box or suitcase to collect their work. Follow the Suitcase Stories on Facebook. Peggy hopes you will enjoy the Suitcase Stories and want to collect the entire series.

www.mascotbooks.com

The Fall Suitcase Stories

For more information, please contact:
Mascot Books
560 Herndon Parkway #120
Herndon, VA 20170
info@mascotbooks.com

Library of Congress Control Number: 2017902535

CPSIA Code: PRT0517A
ISBN-13 :978-1-68401-113-1

Printed in the United States

The Fall Suitcase Stories

Pick me, please

written by Margaret "Peggy" Rose Dolan, Ph.D.

illustrated by Yulia Potts

Penelope, the Pint-Sized Pumpkin

Pitiful, pint-sized Penelope was
Parked in a pumpkin patch.
Pondering her puny size, she
Prescribed to those who passed...

"Pick me, please! Pick me
For a pumpkin pie!
Pick me, please? Pick me?"

Unfortunately, unpumpkins usually paused
Until unanimously they surmised,
Undoubtedly, that Penelope Pumpkin
Understandably was too small in size!

"Pick me, please! Pick me
For a pumpkin pie!
Pick me, please? Pick me?"

Marvin, the Monday market man,
Marked Penelope "morbidly mutated."
Merry mothers meandering by
Mused, "She'd look much better masqueraded!"

"Pick me, please! Pick me
For a pumpkin pie!
Pick me, please? Pick me?"

Poor Penelope proposed a plan, and
Piled the pumpkins pyramid-icaly.
Perching herself at the top point, she claimed,
"People will think I'm the biggest positiv-icaly!"

"Pick me, please! Pick me
For a pumpkin pie!
Pick me, please? Pick me?"

Kind Kelly, the kitchen maid,
Caught a glimpse of Penelope's caper.
Cautiously, Kelly chose coy Penelope,
Crooning, "What shall I carefully make her?"

"A pumpkin pie please!
A pumpkin pie!"

Indescribable was the innocent gleam
In the impish Penelope's eye.
Importantly, Penelope instructed,
"Indubitably, I'll be a pie!"

Naturally, Kelly nodded.
"Not only a pumpkin pie you'll be!
Notch a nook in your neck is what I'll do.
Now night trick-or-treaters can see!"

Timothy and Tobias:
A Thanksgiving Turkey Tale

Just two days before Thanksgiving,
While the last of the autumn leaves burned,
The teacher announced to her attentive class,
"Tomorrow is Timothy's Show & Tell turn!"

Timothy went home considering
What to bring for Show & Tell.
"Everyone's seen a basketball
And a slow turtle's speckled shell!

I want something different,
More spectacular than all the rest,
So my teacher will say, 'Of all the things shown,
Timothy, yours is definitely the best!'

Mom, Mom, what can I bring?
Let's search the house high and low
And find the rarest thing of all,
Something remarkable for me to show!"

"Not in the house," suggested his mom.
"Perhaps in the barnyard you will find
Any one of a number of animals
Just right for Show & Tell time!"

"A pig would be different!" said Timothy,
"But a little messy, I'm afraid.
How about our prized hen
And all the eggs she has laid?

How about my pony Tony?
I could give the kids a ride!
But it'd be hard to keep him in the classroom.
I'd have to tie him up outside!

I could always bring our dog
And Queenie could do all her tricks!
Oh! The teacher said no more dogs
After Eddie Reilly's dog got sick.

Oh Mom, it seems as though
I can't think of one grand thing.
I'm going out to my tire
To think some more while I swing!"

Swinging in the cool, crisp breeze,
Timothy pushed himself high.
Looking over the barnyard scene,
Something colorful caught his eye.

Mom said to look in our backyard,
And sure enough, she was right.
Won't our blue ribbon turkey
Be the most colorful Show & Tell sight?

"Oh, Mom, what an idea!
I know just what to bring!
I've just decided that Tobias Turkey
Is the best of all Show & Tell things!

His colorful feathers and gobbledy song
Will certainly make the kids listen.
If that's not enough, I'll show them
All his Royal Blue County Fair ribbons!"

"Well, Timothy, it's November time,
And because Tobias is such a winner,
Your dad is getting ready to make him
Our Thanksgiving dinner!"

Timothy couldn't believe it
That night as he tried to sleep.
He felt bad about eating Tobias for dinner,
Plus he still didn't have anything unique.

"I've got it! If I can't bring Tobias,
At least I can bring his blue ribbon
And a turkey feather for each kid in class
To help celebrate Thanksgiving!"

So Timothy grabbed some big scissors
And quietly snuck to the barn.
He skillfully cut Tobias's feathers
Until every last one was gone.

The next morn, Timothy dressed for school
And ate his breakfast meal.
His mom said, "Timothy, don't be sad,
We know how you feel."

"So Dad decided to choose another turkey
A little smaller in size,
And you can take Tobias to school
And show off your county fair prize."

"But Mom, what's a turkey
Without feathers on his back?"
"Different," Timothy's mom answered,
"Now what are you hiding in that sack?"

"All of Tobias's turkey feathers.
I cut them off last night.
Now I must bring a featherless turkey
    to school!
What an un-colorful sight!"

"If it weren't for imagination, my son,
Life would be a bore.
You have a while before school begins,
You can think of something for sure!"

"It's back to my swing," sighed Timothy,
Humming a downhearted tune.
But as he pushed on his tire, he screamed,
"Hey Mom, my birthday balloons!"

Mom and Timothy blew and blew,
As fast as they possibly could,
All different colors of balloons.
"I think this will be just as good."

Tobias donned the colorful balloons
All tied to string and taped to his back,
And Timothy wore the blue ribbon
While passing feathers out of his sack.

As the children applauded, the teacher announced
That in all of her teaching career,
The best Show & Tell she'd ever seen
Was by Timothy this very year.

Freddy the Christmas Snowflake

High up in the sky somewhere,
There sailed a great white cloud.
Over the oceans and mountains and lands
It could be seen from all around.

Inside of this great white cloud
Lived snowflakes large and small.
And when the weather turned really cold,
All of the snowflakes would fall.

One small snowflake, Tiny Freddy,
Cried and cried all day.
For the weather was cold and winter was here,
And it was time to go away.

Other snowflakes had told Freddy
That his traveling time would come.
He would pack his bag, say goodbye,
And down to Earth he'd run.

"I don't want to go," cried Freddy.
"No one will like me down there.
I've heard flakes say that I'll be shoveled up!
People will step on me. I'm scared."

Grandfather Flake, who was wise and tall,
Sat little Freddy down.
He told him good things about traveling
        to Earth,
And begged him not to frown.

"You'll see the beauty of the world
Like no other earthling has seen.
You'll see trees from the top and tips of waves,
And the sun will make you gleam.

You might be part of a ski slope,
Or a snowman round and fat,
Or a great big snow castle, grand and royal.
Now, how would you like that?

I hear tell of a great event
That will make this the happiest time to fall,
For Christ the Lord will soon be born.
Men will stand 'round him in awe.

Yet no one will house the Babe.
He will be sleeping in the cold, dark night.
By His crib, perchance, you'll fall
And sparkle for Him bright!

You'll finish the paintings for winter.
You'll add white to cold, grey days.
You'll lift the spirits of little ones.
You'll bring them out to play.

Then, when the wintertime goes,
You'll melt into land, sea, and air.
You'll be sent back to a cloud again,
And be eager to return down there."

"But, Grandfather Flake, I don't know how
To be any of the things you've told.
Maybe I should stay here awhile
And not go down til I'm old."

ATTENTION: FREDDY FLAKE, REPORT PLEASE
WITH YOUR BAGGAGE IN YOUR HAND.
SAY YOUR GOODBYES, GET IN LINE,
YOU'RE GOING TO TRAVEL TO LAND.

"I don't want to go, I don't want to go.
I'll never, never leave.
Can't I stay? Can't I stay?
Oh, why did they pick me?"

"Because," said Grandfather Flake,
In a voice loud and stern,
"This has always been a snowflake's life,
And it happens to be your turn!

Now, be on your way.
Don't worry, little one, you'll learn as you go.
Be yourself! The rest will come.
You'll learn soon how to be snow!"

"Goodbye, goodbye, Grandfather Flake.
I'm falling, falling fast.
Wow! I've got lots of company.
There goes Frannie Flake flying past.

Look at the trees! Grandfather was right.
I can see everything for miles.
I see mountain tops and lots of people.
Look at all the smiles!"

"There is the star so bright.
It blinds my snowflake goggles.
I see shepherds and kings passing by.
Look! They're heading for that hovel.

So am I! I'm drifting close.
Oh, wherever will I land?
Oh...if Grandfather could see me now!
I'm right next to the baby's hand!

I'm in a painting, on a greeting card,
I'm in a Christmas carol, too.
I'm in a million and one eyes,
And I'm in Christmas hearts, too!"

And so little Freddy learned his lesson
And became part of our Christmas scenery.
His story is told to other flakes now.
He's part of Snowflake History!

About the Author
Margaret "Peggy" Rose Dolan, Ph.D.

Photograph by Tiffany Bickel

During Peggy Dolan's 44-year career in education, she proudly answered to the titles of teacher, principal, professor, and author. A highlight of her career came when she was a principal. She developed a program to reduce fighting and bullying in her school and was the founder and president of Fight Free Schools in 1993. By 1998, she was invited by then-First Lady Hillary Clinton to the first White House Conference on School Violence. Peggy authored a textbook, now in its second edition, entitled *Fight Free Schools: Creating A School Culture That Promotes Achievement,* published by Rising Sun Publishing. She has been recognized for her positive contributions to children, teachers, and the community by receiving several awards from the St. Louis County Government and Family Courts. Her Fight Free Schools Program was recognized as a promising school program for preventing violence in schools by Attorney General Janet Reno in the Annual Report on School Violence in 1998.

Now, as Aunt Peggy the Storyteller, she holds story sessions at Faust Park in St. Louis, Missouri, and various libraries and schools in the region. During these sessions, Peggy encourages the students to participate with a variety of puppets and props she has in her old suitcase. All of her stories are written in poetic form and involve characters who share the challenges that all kids face as they grow up. Utilizing the tools that come with strength of character, perseverance, and teamwork, her characters arrive at playful but solid solutions that will steer them true on their journey in life. Aunt Peggy loves to spend time with her 9 nieces and 12 great nieces and nephews, whom she lovingly refers to as her Angels of God.

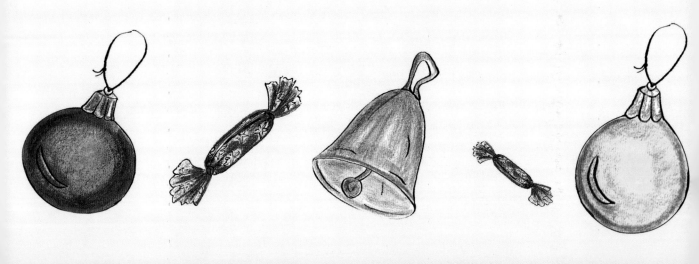

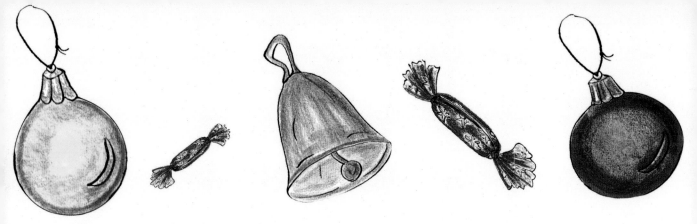

MASCOT® BOOKS

Have a book idea?
Contact us at:

info@mascotbooks.com | www.mascotbooks.com

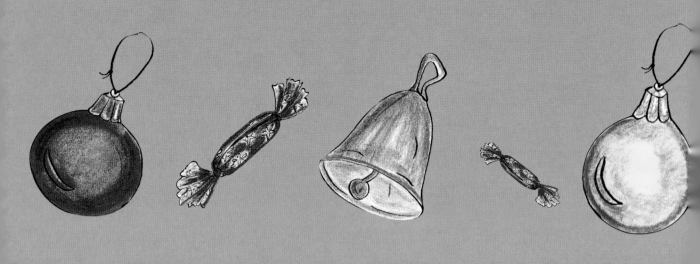